THE HAPPY LIONESS

THE HAPPY LIONESS

by Louise Fatio

pictures by Roger Duvoisin

McGraw-Hill Book Company

NEW YORK   ST. LOUIS   SAN FRANCISCO   TORONTO   LONDON   SYDNEY

The copyright and Library of Congress data appear on the last page.

THE HAPPY LION and his Lioness were fond of their zoo house and their garden where birds and squirrels came to play in the trees.

The Happy Lion loved to sit on top of the garden's biggest rock. From this high place he had a fine view of the zoo's gardens and of the visitors who strolled along the paths.

But, one day, as he jumped down from the rock he hit a loose stone, fell, and broke a paw.

Unhappy Happy Lion! He was taken to the animal hospital to have his paw mended.

The Lioness remained alone in the zoo. Unhappy Lioness! She was so sad to be without her Happy Lion.

Yet, she was amused. She saw that while the Happy Lion was away very, very few people stopped around the moat to look at her and greet her.

"People are so queer," she laughed. "They do not care for me because I have no mane. No mane, no lion. Only a dull, bare-headed creature!"

"Of course," said her friend the Raven. "These visitors think you are not a Lion. They say: LIONS ARE BEAUTIFUL KINGLY ANIMALS. They never say: LIONESSES ARE BEAUTIFUL QUEENLY ANIMALS. But I have an idea: we can make a fine mane for you with the fresh tall grasses that grow in the fields around here. Then you will be a glorious LION!"

"Yes, let's do it," cried the Squirrels, the Ducks, the Rabbits, the Blue Jay, and the Lioness's other friends.

"That would be so funny," laughed the Lioness.

So, all her friends ran or flew to the fields and gardens to pick the long grasses and flowers and bring them back to the lions' rock garden.

Then they wove a rich mane of grasses and flowers around the Lioness's head and neck. No lion had ever had such a brilliant and colorful mane. How delighted and amused the Lioness was when she looked at herself in the clear water of the moat.

"The visitors will no longer think I am just a poor Lioness when they see me," she said with a laugh.

Why, indeed, the path around the moat became more crowded with visitors than it had ever been. They saluted the NOBLE FLOWERY LION with cries of admiration. The Lioness was now the glorious and beloved LION. And how she laughed.

But now François, the zoo keeper's son, came to see the Lioness. "My dear Lioness," he said, "you have fun with that mane, but the grasses and flowers are fading fast. You will again be only a Lioness. I think the grasses and flowers should be replaced by a mane of real hair that will never fade. Then you will have more fun looking like a true, proud LION."

François was wise. He found packs of long hairs at three shops of hairdressers he knew. He brought the hair and some colorful rolls of string just as the mane of flowers was falling down.

With the help of the Raven and other friends, François wove a rich mane for the Lioness and tied it on her. "No lion ever looked as kingly as you do now," François assured her.

Never had so many visitors gathered to admire
the most KINGLY LION they had ever seen. And never

had the Lioness had so much fun, or been so happy.
She was now the most glorious inhabitant of the zoo.

But now, with his paw as good as new, the Happy Lion was brought back to his house and rock garden.

What a surprise awaited him!

Who was this long-maned Lion who stood proudly on the biggest rock? Had he been brought there to replace the Happy Lion?

And where was his Lioness?

He was angry and ready to fight the newcomer.

How amazed he was when that long-maned LION ran down to him and rubbed his hairy head against his own!

"HOH!" the Happy Lion suddenly exclaimed, "you are my Lioness."

"Yes, my Happy Lion," answered the Lioness. "I am your Happy Lioness."

"But, oh dear, how did that big mane ever grow on you? It is twice as big as mine!"

The Happy Lioness explained how all this had happened.

How the Happy Lion laughed!

"If our visitors love you so much because of your fine mane you should keep it," he said. "It looks so nice on you."

"No," said the Lioness. "I want to be a Lioness again, a Happy Lioness. And now that you are back it would be silly to continue the joke on the visitors."

Saying this, she began to pull off her mane with the help of her friends. Soon she was a real LIONESS, bare head and all.

She cuddled her head against her Happy Lion's mane, saying, "I love you. I am *your* Happy Lioness."

"I love you, too," answered the Happy Lion. "I am *your* Happy Lion."

And all the visitors around the moat applauded and blew kisses at them.

Library of Congress Cataloging in Publication Data

Fatio, Louise.   The happy lioness.
  Summary: While the Happy Lion is at the animal
hospital, the Happy Lioness receives help from her
friends in attracting visitors who only like to see
a lion with a full mane.
  [1. Lions—Fiction] I. Duvoisin, Roger Antoine,
1904-   II. Title.
PZ7.F268Han   [E]   80-11258
ISBN 0-07-020069-6

Copyright © 1980 by Louise Fatio Duvoisin and Roger Duvoisin.
All Rights Reserved. Printed in the United States of America.
No part of this publication may be reproduced, stored in a
retrieval system, or transmitted, in any form or by any means,
electronic, mechanical, photocopying, recording, or otherwise,
without the prior written permission of the publisher.

1 2 3 4 5 6 7 8 9   R A B P   8 7 6 5 4 3 2 1 0